# Mary *and* Her Little Lamb

Dear Reader,

Growing up, the poem and song "Mary Had a Little Lamb" was an iconic building block of my early days, as I suspect it is for most children. Not that I worried about it much as a child, but I never dreamed that the poem was based on an actual young girl and her little lamb. It was not until some years ago, when I was well past my happy childhood, and while attending a showing of my paintings at a gallery near Sudbury, Massachusetts, that I discovered by chance the actual schoolhouse Mary and the lamb attended (now located on the site of the famous Wayside Inn in Sudbury). It was there at the Wayside Inn site that I began to learn the roots of the story surrounding Mary and her lamb.

I originally thought that the poem likely had its roots in Mother Goose or old European folktales. But no—the people and events leading up to the creation of the poem were, in fact, quite real. The story of Mary and her lamb was actually written down by Mary in her later life and distributed in a charming little pamphlet. It was Mary's own story that was the basis for this book.

How odd it is that an event so simple, so innocent, and so long ago could have been the basis for something that is as steadfastly ingrained in our culture as this poem. I hope you enjoy reading the tale as much as I enjoyed writing and painting it.

Will Moses

# Mary *and* Her Little Lamb

## The True Story of the Famous Nursery Rhyme

WILL MOSES • Philomel Books
An Imprint of Penguin Group (USA) Inc.

Mary had a little lamb,

Its fleece was white as snow,

And everywhere that Mary went

The lamb was sure to go ;

He followed her to school one day—

That was against the rule,

It made the children laugh and play,

To see a lamb at school.

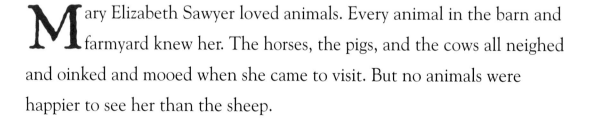

**M**ary Elizabeth Sawyer loved animals. Every animal in the barn and farmyard knew her. The horses, the pigs, and the cows all neighed and oinked and mooed when she came to visit. But no animals were happier to see her than the sheep.

One early morning when she went to the barn with her
father, she found two little lambs in the sheep pen—they
had been born while she was sleeping! They both were tiny,
but one had been born smaller and frailer than the other,
and its mother had turned it away. The little lamb was all
alone, shivering, hungry, and very sick. When she looked
up to Mary with big brown eyes and let out a weak little
baaaaaaaa, it just about broke Mary's heart.

"I'll save you," Mary said as she cuddled the little lamb
in her arms and carried her back to the farmhouse.

"A lamb in the house!" said Mary's mother. "Oh, Mary!"

But Mary hugged the little lamb close. "Please?" she said. "Please, Mother, let me keep her. She's so sick."

Mary begged and pleaded until her mother finally said, "All right then, Mary, but she is your responsibility." Then, with a sigh, she brought the little lamb some of her special catnip tea. Mary's mother wanted the lamb to get better too.

Mary wrapped the lamb in an old linen dress and held her close, feeding her drops of catnip tea all through that dreary March day, worrying all the while. Finally, around suppertime, the little lamb began to swallow the warm milk Mary's father had brought in from the barn, and soon enough, her eyes brightened.

"Oh, little lamb," Mary said, "maybe you will live after all." But deep down Mary still wondered—the lamb was so small and weak.

Mary spent the cold night in front of the fireplace with her little lamb, snuggling with her and keeping her warm. She wasn't sure if the lamb would make it until morning. But when Mary woke up, she was happy to see the lamb was not only alive but was standing up on her sturdy little legs.

In no time at all, the lamb was following Mary everywhere that she went. Down the lane, over the meadow, across the falls, and even into town. "What a dear little lamb you are," Mary said as they ran together down the road.

Mary washed her little lamb, combed out the burrs, and tied pretty ribbons in her wool. The lamb loved Mary too. She would close her eyes and hang her head for Mary so she could brush the lamb's woolly locks.

Once the lamb was well, Mary put her in the pen with the other sheep, but she wouldn't stay! Instead, the little lamb slept in a corner of the woodshed—made especially for her by Mary. And when grazing in the pasture, she preferred the company of horses and cows. "What a dear little lamb," Mary giggled when she saw the lamb playing.

19

On long summer days Mary and her lamb would pick flowers and make daisy chains. Since Mary's friends lived far away, the lamb became her best playmate. Mary would dress up the little lamb and host tea parties in the meadow. The lamb would merrily play along, happy to be with her best friend.

On the first day of school, just as Mary started down the lane, she remembered that she had not said good-bye to her lamb! Mary called out across the meadow, and soon enough, the snow white lamb came running. "What a dear little lamb you are," said Mary with a wave good-bye. "I'll see you when school lets out!"

But as Mary continued on, the lamb was close behind. Through the meadows and over the stone walls, she followed—even when Mary took the shortcut across the narrow footbridge. Before long they were at the schoolhouse. With a look over her shoulder, Mary walked through the schoolroom door . . .

27

And the little lamb followed! She trotted right in, bold and proud, just as if she had always belonged there. She pranced over the worn plank floor, her little black hooves clattering all the way to Mary's desk, where she quickly made herself at home under Mary's seat. Mary tossed a quilt over her little friend to keep her hidden as they settled into the school day.

When Miss Kimball arrived at the school, she had brought with her a visitor, Mr. John Roulstone. By the time Miss Kimball rang the school bell and began the day's lesson, almost all of the children in the school knew there was a lamb under Mary's desk and were trying hard not to laugh.

Soon enough, though, Miss Kimball called on Mary to come to the front of the room to recite the lesson. Mary slowly walked down the aisle, hoping her lamb wouldn't follow. At first, Mary walked alone. But then she heard a click-click-click-click over the floorboards behind her. It was her lamb, wearing the blanket Mary had thrown on top of her. The students cheered, whistled, and laughed—even Miss Kimball and Mary herself could not help but laugh at the sight of the little lamb who had gone to school.

Mr. Roulstone was so amused by the spectacle of the lamb in school that the next morning he returned to the schoolhouse. Calling Mary to him, he handed her a piece of paper upon which he had written:

Mary had a little lamb,
Its fleece was white as snow,
And everywhere that Mary went
The lamb was sure to go;
He followed her to school one day—
That was against the rule,
It made the children laugh and play,
To see a lamb at school.

As the sun set later that evening, Mary gathered her family around and recited the poem for everyone to hear. And all the while, she wove colored ribbons through the woolly locks of her happy, contented, and now famous little lamb.

# Mary Had a Little Lamb

Ma-ry had a lit-tle lamb, lit-tle lamb, lit-tle lamb, Ma-ry had a lit-tle lamb, its

fleece was white as snow; And ev'-ry-where that Ma-ry went, Ma-ry went, Ma-ry went, ev'-ry-where that

Ma-ry went, the lamb was sure to go. It fol-lowed her to school one day, school one day, school one day, It

fol-lowed her to school one day, which was a-gainst the rule; It made the chil-dren laugh and play,

laugh and play, laugh and play, It made the chil-dren laugh and play, to see a lamb at school.

And so the teacher turned it out,
But still it lingered near,
And waited patiently about
Till Mary did appear.

"Why does the lamb love Mary so?"
The eager children cry;
"Why, Mary loves the lamb,
You know," the teacher did reply.

Mary Elizabeth Sawyer was born in 1806 in Sterling, Massachusetts. She attended the Redstone Schoolhouse in Sudbury, Massachusetts. According to many sources, in the 1810s John Roulstone visited and saw Mary and her little lamb, much the way it's described in this story. It is said that he delivered the first stanza of the poem that we know of as "Mary Had a Little Lamb" to Mary at school the next day. Later, in 1830, a writer and editor named Sarah Josepha Hale published the poem and is said to have added three more stanzas to the one that John Roulstone wrote. Soon after that, Lowell Mason, a famous American musician who composed more than 1600 hymns, put the poem to music and added in the repetition of the words that we sing today. He taught music in public schools in Massachusetts, was co-founder of the Boston Academy of Music, and was music superintendent for the Boston school system. It's not clear how the song became as popular as it has, but it's now one of the first songs that many people learn when they start playing the piano. And it's all because of a sweet girl named Mary and one dear little lamb!

To Patti Gauch—thank you for having faith

## PHILOMEL BOOKS

A division of Penguin Young Readers Group.   Published by The Penguin Group.   Penguin Group (USA) Inc., 375 Hudson Street, New York, NY 10014, U.S.A.
Penguin Group (Canada), 90 Eglinton Avenue East, Suite 700, Toronto, Ontario M4P 2Y3, Canada (a division of Pearson Penguin Canada Inc.).
Penguin Books Ltd, 80 Strand, London WC2R 0RL, England.   Penguin Ireland, 25 St. Stephen's Green, Dublin 2, Ireland (a division of Penguin Books Ltd).
Penguin Group (Australia), 250 Camberwell Road, Camberwell, Victoria 3124, Australia (a division of Pearson Australia Group Pty Ltd).
Penguin Books India Pvt Ltd, 11 Community Centre, Panchsheel Park, New Delhi - 110 017, India.
Penguin Group (NZ), 67 Apollo Drive, Rosedale, North Shore 0632, New Zealand (a division of Pearson New Zealand Ltd).
Penguin Books (South Africa) (Pty) Ltd, 24 Sturdee Avenue, Rosebank, Johannesburg 2196, South Africa.
Penguin Books Ltd, Registered Offices: 80 Strand, London WC2R 0RL, England.

Design by Semadar Megged.   Text set in 16-point Goudy Old Style BT.   The art was done in oil on Fabriano paper.

Library of Congress Cataloging-in-Publication Data
Moses, Will. Mary and her little lamb : the true story of the nursery rhyme / Will Moses.   p. cm.
Summary: In 1810s Massachusetts, young Mary Elizabeth Sawyer nurses a sickly lamb back to health and becomes the subject of a famous
nursery rhyme. Includes facts about the real Mary, John Roulstone who wrote the rhyme, and Lowell Mason who set it to music.
[1. Sheep—Fiction. 2. Animals—Infancy—Fiction. 3. Farm life—Massachusetts—Fiction. 4. Schools—Fiction.
5. Massachusetts—History—1775–1865—Fiction.] I. Title.  PZ7.M8477Mar 2011  [E]—dc22  2010037445
ISBN 978-0-399-25154-2
Special Markets ISBN 978-0-399-25573-1 Not for resale
3 5 7 9 10 8 6 4 2

This Imagination Library edition is published by Penguin Group (USA), a Pearson
company, exclusively for Dolly Parton's Imagination Library, a not-for-profit
program designed to inspire a love of reading and learning, sponsored in part by The
Dollywood Foundation. Penguin's trade editions of this work are available wherever
books are sold.